Karen's School Mystery

**Look for these
and other books about Karen
in the
Baby-sitters Little Sister series:**

Little Sister

Karen's School Mystery
Ann M. Martin

Illustrations by Susan Tang

A
LITTLE APPLE
PAPERBACK

SCHOLASTIC INC.
New York Toronto London Auckland Sydney

No part of this publication may be reproduced in whole or in part, or stored in a retrieval system, or transmitted in any form or by any means, electronic, mechanical, photocopying, recording, or otherwise, without written permission of the publisher. For information regarding permission, write to Scholastic Inc., 555 Broadway, New York, NY 10012.

ISBN 0-590-48303-X

12 11 10 9 8 7 6 5   8 9 0/09

Printed in the U.S.A.   40

First Scholastic printing, January 1995

Karen's School Mystery

January

"Hi, Hannie! Hi, Hannie!" I called. It was January, and I was happy to be back at school after our vacation.

"Hi, Karen!" Hannie called back. "Hi, Nancy!" Hannie Papadakis ran to meet my friend Nancy Dawes and me.

I am Karen Brewer. Hannie and Nancy and I are *best* friends. We call ourselves the Three Musketeers. We like their motto, which is *One for all and all for one.*

My friends and I ran to the front door of our school. When we reached it, we had to stop running. That was because of the Red Brigade. The Red Brigade are the patrols at Stoneybrook Academy. They are students, they get to wear cool badges and belts, and they are posted everywhere inside and out-side of school. The inside ones always tell kids not to run in the halls.

I think the patrols' badges are gigundoly cool.

"Guess what," said Hannie as we walked slowly by a hallway patrol. (We did not want to be reported to the principal.) "It is almost time to elect new patrols."

Hannie was right. The kids at our school only get to be patrols for a month. Then we choose new ones. This is because lots of kids want to be patrols. More of them get turns this way.

"Maybe I'll run for the Red Brigade this time," I said. Anyone in second grade or higher can be a patrol. I had not thought much about it before. But now I decided I would like one of those badges. Also, I would like to be in charge.

"I will nominate you, Karen," said Nancy grandly.

"Thank you," I replied.

Nancy and Hannie and I are in second grade here at Stoneybrook Academy. We are seven years old. Our teacher is Ms. Colman, and we love her. (I even got to be a co-flower girl in her wedding.)

Hannie and Nancy and I walked into our classroom. Ms. Colman wasn't there yet, but some other kids were. And the door was open between our room and Mr. Berger's room next door. I knew Mr. Berger was keeping an eye on us.

My friends and I put our things in our cubbies. Then we sat on some desks in the back of the room. Hannie and Nancy get to sit back there all the time, but not me. My desk is in the front row. That is because I wear glasses. Ms. Colman makes all the glasses-wearers sit near the blackboard. I guess Ms. Colman has a right to make up that rule. She is a glasses-wearer herself. (Plus, she is the teacher.) So I sit between

3

Ricky Torres and Natalie Springer.

Nancy and Hannie and I watched our classmates trickle in. We saw Pamela Harding, Jannie Gilbert, and Leslie Morris. They are another set of best friends. And sometimes they are the Three Musketeers' best enemies. We saw Addie Sidney roll into the room in her wheelchair. We saw Ricky Torres. Ricky is my pretend husband. We got married on the playground one day. We saw the twins, Tammy and Terri Barkan. We saw Audrey Green and Chris Lamar and Vicky Anders. We saw Bobby Gianelli. Bobby lives on my street. I used to think he was a bully, but now we are sort of friends.

Bobby hung up his coat and went to his desk. He stuck his hand inside it. He felt around. Then he leaned over and peered inside. "Hey!" he cried. "My candy bar is gone! It disappeared."

Now this was interesting. Everyone crowded around Bobby's desk. We asked questions. We looked for the candy bar. We

even dumped out the stuff in his desk. But the candy bar really was gone.

When Ms. Colman arrived, she looked at the mess on the floor. And she looked at all of us. We were talking a mile a minute.

"What a way to start the new year," she said. But she did not sound cross with us for making a mess. Ms. Colman is the best teacher ever.

Nancy's Wish

We never did find Bobby's candy bar. (He had probably taken it home with him before vacation, and forgot.) Instead, we had a regular old January day at school. We read stories. We worked in our workbooks. We ate lunch in the cafeteria. We had to have recess in our classroom, though. Ms. Colman said the weather was too cold for playing on the playground.

When school was over, Nancy and I rode home on the bus. (Hannie rides the bus, too, but she takes a different route.) While we were bouncing along, Nancy said to me, "You know what, Karen? I wish I could be more grown-up."

"What do you mean?" I asked.

"I mean . . . I mean . . ." Nancy paused. "I mean I wish I looked more grown-up. I wish my hair were shorter. And I wish my clothes were not so babyish. Also, I wish Mommy and Daddy would treat me like I was older. After all, I am seven going on eight."

"You want to get your hair cut?" I said.

Nancy nodded. "Yup. And I want to get rid of these old baby-baby pink sneakers and this skirt with the suspenders."

"If you do get your hair cut," I said, "remember *not* to go to Gloriana's House of Hair."

"Oh, don't worry," replied Nancy. "I would never do that."

Nancy and I were thinking about the time I got a haircut at Gloriana's. It was a disaster. I looked like a squirrel. Now my hair has grown back. It is very long again.

Our bus bounced along. Finally it reached our stop. Nancy ran to her house, and I ran to mine. (We live next door to each other.)

"Hi, everybody! I am home!" I yelled.

"Indoor voice, Karen!" called Mommy.

This is one thing you should know about me: Sometimes, my voice gets a little loud. Grown-ups are always reminding me to use my quiet indoor voice.

Here are some other things you should know about me: I talk a lot, too. I have blonde hair, blue eyes, and some freckles. I wear glasses. (I have two pairs. The blue pair is for reading. The pink pair is for the rest of the time.) I live in Stoneybrook, Connecticut. I have two families. They are my little-house family and my big-house family. (I will tell you more about my two families later.)

The house I was in now was the little house. That meant I was at Mommy's. I found Mommy and my little brother Andrew reading a story in the living room.

Even though Andrew is only four going on five, he can already read. (Guess who taught him. I did.) So he was reading to Mommy. He was reading to her about the pokey little puppy while Mommy cleaned up her desk.

When I entered the living room, Andrew stopped reading. "Hi," he said. "What did you do in school today?"

Lately Andrew always wants to know what I did in school. That is because he wishes he could go to Stoneybrook Academy instead of preschool. I can understand that (even though he does have a gigundoly nice preschool teacher named Miss Jewel).

"Well," I said, "we worked on math problems — subtraction mostly — and we read stories called tall tales. We had recess inside and we played board games. And in art class we are making mobiles. Um, Bobby Gianelli lost a candy bar. Oh, and I made an important decision."

"About what?"

"I will announce it at dinner," I replied.

The Red Brigade

All afternoon, Andrew pestered me. He wanted to know what my big decision was. I made him wait until dinner.

At dinner I said, "Okay, everybody, I will now announce my decision."

"Yes?" said Mommy and Seth. (Seth is my stepfather.)

"Goody," said Andrew.

"I have decided," I began, "to be a patrol. I am going to run for the Red Brigade. I will get to wear a badge."

"Cool," said Andrew. (Andrew has a police officer's badge and a sheriff's badge. They are very special to him.)

My little-house family seemed proud of my decision. So I thought that after supper I should call my big-house family and tell them the news, too. And now, maybe I better tell you about my two families.

This is the first thing you should know: I did not always have two families. A long time ago, when I was just a little kid, I had only one family. Mommy, Daddy, Andrew, and me. We lived together in a big house, the house Daddy grew up in. (It is right here in Stoneybrook, not too far from the little house.) We used to be a happy family, but then Mommy and Daddy began to fight. They fought a *lot*. Finally they decided to get a divorce. They decided they could not live together anymore. After the divorce, Mommy moved to the little house, and Daddy stayed in the big house. And sometime after that, they got married again. But not to each other. Mommy married Seth, and Daddy married Elizabeth. And that is how Andrew and I wound up with two families. We go back and forth between them — a month at the big house, a month at the little house. And at the beginning of each year, we switch the months so that, for instance, we are not *always* at the big house in November for Thanksgiving, or *always* at the little house in December for Christmas.

Here is who lives at the little house: Mommy, Seth, Andrew, me, Rocky, Midgie, Emily Junior, and Bob. Rocky and Midgie are Seth's cat and dog. Emily Junior is my pet rat. Bob is Andrew's hermit crab.

Here is who lives at the big house: Daddy, Elizabeth, Charlie, Sam, David Michael, Kristy, Emily Michelle, Nannie, Andrew, me, Boo-Boo, Shannon, Goldfishie and Crystal Light, and Emily Junior and Bob. (Emily Junior and Bob go back and forth with Andrew and me). In case you are wondering, Charlie, Sam, David Michael, and Kristy are my stepbrothers and stepsister. (They are Elizabeth's kids. She

13

was married once before she married Daddy.) Emily Michelle is my special adopted sister. Daddy and Elizabeth adopted her from the faraway country of Vietnam. Nannie is Elizabeth's mother. She helps take care of the kids and the house. Boo-Boo is Daddy's fat old cat, Shannon is David Michael's puppy, and Goldfishie and Crystal Light are goldfish (duh).

Do you know what? I made up special nicknames for my brother and me. I call us Andrew Two-Two and Karen Two-Two. (I thought up those names after Ms. Colman read a book to our class. It was called *Jacob Two-Two Meets the Hooded Fang*.) We are two-twos because we have two of so many things. We have two houses and two families, two mommies and two daddies, two cats and two dogs. I have two bicycles, one at each house. (Andrew has two trikes.) I have two stuffed cats that look just the same. Moosie stays at the big house. Goosie stays at the little house. And Andrew and I have clothes and books and toys at each

14

house. (This is so we will not have to pack much when we go back and forth.) Plus I have my two best friends. (Nancy lives next to the little house, and Hannie lives across from the big house.) And of course I have those two pairs of glasses. I like being a two-two (most of the time).

As a two-two, I get to do a lot of things twice. So after dinner, I called my big-house family to tell *them* about the Red Brigade.

Here is what Kristy said: "Go for it, Karen!"

Missing

Ms. Colman makes lots of announcements in our classroom. Sometimes she makes Surprising Announcements. Those are my favorites. The day after I called Kristy, Ms. Colman made an announcement to our class. But it was just a regular one. It was not surprising. This was because it was about the Red Brigade. My classmates and I already know everything about being elected a patrol. We have heard the announcement once a month since school started.

"As you know," Ms. Colman began, "the election of new patrols will be held tomorrow. So think about who you would like to nominate."

"Goody," said a voice from behind me. I think it was Bobby Gianelli. This was very silly because Bobby had already been a patrol.

Maybe I better tell you a little more about the Red Brigade. See, once a month, two students from every class are chosen to be new patrols. (Well, not in *every* class. The kindergarteners and the first-graders are too little. But in every class from second grade up.) The patrols are in charge of a lot of things in the morning before school starts, and in the afternoon until the buses leave. They make sure kids don't run in the halls. They help the littlest kids to their buses. And if they see any problems — such as fighting, or big kids picking on little kids, or breaking *any* rules — they can report kids to Mrs. Noonan. (She is in charge of the Red Brigade.) They can even report kids to Mrs. Titus, our principal, if there is an emergency. Each patrol is assigned a post — a hallway or a doorway or a bus or something — and he or she is in charge of that post for a month. At the end of the month, new patrols are chosen. Guess what. When the Red Brigade changes, a very important badge ceremony is held. Mrs. Noonan, the new patrols, the old patrols, and the parents of the old patrols are invited to the auditorium. Then Mrs. Titus thanks the old patrols for doing such a good job and for being such good citizens. And *then* (and this is gigundoly special) the old patrols take off their badges and belts and put them on the new patrols. The parents are very proud.

Ms. Colman finished reminding us about the elections. "As you know," she was saying, "we will elect just two patrols tomorrow. You may nominate yourself, or whomever you want — but you may not nominate someone who has already been a patrol. And remember, if you are nominated tomorrow and you do not win, you will have another chance next month. Any questions?"

No one had a question, since we have heard the speech so often. But on the playground we talked about the elections. The Three Musketeers huddled next to the school (it was still pretty cold outside) with Addie, Natalie, Bobby, and Ricky. We talked about who wanted to run for the Red Brigade, and who had already been a patrol.

Suddenly I remembered something. "Hey, Bobby," I said. "Did you ever find your candy bar?"

"Nope," he replied.

He hadn't found it? I was sure it was at his house.

"You know what?" said Addie. "Liddie Yuan left a quarter in her desk and now it is missing." (Liddie is in Mr. Berger's class.)

"A bunch of things have disappeared

from kids' desks since yesterday," spoke up Hannie. "Linny said so." (Linny is Hannie's big brother. He is in fourth grade at Stoneybrook Academy.)

Hmm. I did not like the sound of that.

The Winners

I felt a little nervous the next day. I had a hard time waiting for Ms. Colman to say, "Okay, girls and boys. Time for elections." I knew Nancy was going to nominate me. But I still felt butterflies in my stomach. Nominating me did not mean I would win.

At last Ms. Colman told us to put away our science books. She faced our class. It was election time.

Ms. Colman picked up a piece of chalk. "Who would like to nominate someone to join the Red Brigade?" she asked. Nancy must have shot her hand up right away, because Ms. Colman said, "Yes, Nancy?"

"I nominate Karen Brewer," Nancy said importantly.

"Karen Brewer," Ms. Colman repeated. She wrote my name on the board. Then she looked around the room. "Anyone else?"

Audrey Green raised her hand. "I nominate Vicky Anders," she said.

Ms. Colman added Vicky's name to the list. "Anyone else?"

Addie raised her hand. "I nominate myself."

Ms. Colman nodded. As she was writing Addie's name, I heard whispering behind me. I guess Ms. Colman heard it, too. When she turned around again, she said, "Does somebody have something to share with the rest of us?"

Leslie Morris squirmed in her seat. "Well, I was just wondering," she began. "I mean, Addie is in a wheelchair." She paused. "I mean . . ."

I glanced at Addie. She sits in her wheel-

chair at the end of a row of desks. She does not need a desk of her own because she writes on the lapboard that is attached to the side of her chair. It is like her own portable desk. And she carries everything she needs in a tote bag on the back of her chair.

Addie has cerebral palsy. She cannot walk because her legs do not work the way mine do. But her arms do. And her head does. And her brain does. Addie can do most things I can do (and a few I can't). And she can scoot around pretty fast in her chair.

I glared at Leslie. I had a feeling I knew what she was thinking. So did Addie. "I can be a patrol," said Addie quietly.

"But you cannot walk. Or run," said Leslie.

"I can *move*," Addie pointed out.

Natalie raised her hand. "Ms. Colman, what if Addie saw a kid running in the hall? What would she do?"

Addie answered for herself. "I would do

what any patrol would do," she said. "I would yell, 'No running!' If I had to, I would report the kid."

That was the end of the discussion. After that, Tammy Barkan nominated her sister Terri. And then Ms. Colman said, "Okay. Heads down, boys and girls. Time to vote."

Each of us raised our hand to vote for one person. When Ms. Colman said, "Heads up," I looked at the board. This is what I saw:

Karen Brewer – 6   Addie Sidney – 6

Vicky Anders – 4   Terri Barkan – 2

Addie and I had won! We were the new patrols!

Karen's Badge

Two days later, I was standing on the stage in our school auditorium. Next to me was Addie. We were in a row of new patrols. On the other side of the stage was the row of old patrols. Among them were Chris Lamar and Jannie Gilbert, from my class. The old patrols were wearing their badges. In the center of the stage were Mrs. Titus and Mrs. Noonan. And in the audience were the parents of the old patrols. They were there to watch their kids put their badges on the new patrols, and to hear

Mrs. Titus congratulate them. The parents looked very, very proud.

Mrs. Titus began to speak. "Thank you for coming here this afternoon," she said. "And thank you, patrols, for the wonderful job you have done. You have shown the other students how to be good citizens. You have worked hard. We congratulate you."

The parents clapped then. They clapped loudly. They were smiling. I smiled, too. I was thinking that in one month *my* parents would be here. And they would be clapping for me.

After Mrs. Titus' speech, the new patrols walked across the stage, one by one. And one by one, they took off their belts and badges and put them on the new patrols. A second-grade patrol named Colleen slipped her belt over my head. I looked down at it. My own patrol badge. I was now a member of the Red Brigade for one month.

After the ceremony, Mrs. Noonan asked the patrols, old and new, to meet with her for a few minutes. We sat in a classroom. Mrs. Noonan said, "Okay, boys and girls. First I will assign the new patrols to their posts. Second-graders and third-graders will work in pairs."

Mrs. Noonan read from a list. Addie and I were going to be partners. We were going to be in charge of an intersection. That is a place where one hallway crosses another hallway. It was an important post because it was very busy. As Mrs. Noonan said, "Lots of traffic." (She meant kids, not cars.) I knew Addie and I would be calling out, "Walk, don't run" a lot.

After Mrs. Noonan had assigned our posts, she said, "Now this afternoon — and only this afternoon — the old patrols will work with you new patrols. They will show you what you need to know about your posts. They will tell you what to do."

That afternoon, Addie and I felt very special. That was because we were allowed to leave our classroom five minutes before the bell rang. And we got to put on our badges first.

Addie and I arrived proudly at our post — the hallway intersection. We met Colleen. Carter Lewis was there, too. He had been another second-grade patrol. (They are in Mr. Berger's class.)

Colleen took charge. "Now as soon as the bell rings," she said, "the halls will be filled with kids. You have to keep a special eye on the kindergarteners. Their classrooms are right over there, and sometimes they need help with things."

The bell rang then, and Colleen was right. Suddenly kids were everywhere.

"Hey, no running!" called Carter.

The kid Carter yelled at stopped running. But he looked angry.

Colleen hurried over to some kids at the water fountain. "Make a *line*!" she said. "I told you before. Make a line. Or," she added, "I will report you."

Colleen turned to me. Two of the kids at the fountain made faces at her back. I glanced at Addie. Addie raised her eyebrows at me. I made another decision. I was going to be a nice patrol. Not a mean one like Colleen or Carter.

On the Job

On Monday morning, I hopped off the school bus. I hurried to my post in the hallway. Addie was already there. Her bus had arrived before mine did. I put on my badge. Then I grinned at Addie. "Ready to work?" I asked her.

Addie nodded importantly. "Yup."

The hallway was already getting crowded. Kids were streaming to their classrooms. Some went into the bathrooms or to the office. Some were looking for teachers. The kids were noisy. They shouted to each other. They tossed things in the air. One kid threw a wad of paper on the floor.

"No littering!" called Addie sharply. "Pick that up!"

Even though the kid was a big fifth-grader, he picked up the paper. But then he walked behind Addie and stuck his tongue out at her. I wondered if I should do something. But what? Call out, "No sticking out your tongue"? That seemed silly.

A moment later, two fifth-graders ran by.

"Walk, don't run!" called Addie. "Do you want me to rep — "

I nudged Addie. "Don't," I whispered.

Addie let the kids go. "Why?" she whispered back.

"They are *big* kids," I replied. "We do not want them to hate us. I mean, we are only patrols for a month. After that we are just regular second-graders again. I do not want them to be mean to us later."

"Well . . . okay," replied Addie. But she

did not sound too sure about what I had said.

For awhile, Addie and I just watched the kids. We saw a sixth-grader run around a corner. We saw a fifth-grader tease a third-grader. And then we saw two kindergarteners running. They were running *fast*. And they were heading for some other kids.

"Karen — " Addie began to say.

"Okay, okay," I replied. I snagged the little kids as they flew by me. "Hey! Hey! Walk, don't run! No running in the halls!" I said sharply. "You almost ran into those other kids."

The kindergarteners — two little girls — looked worried.

"Are you going to report us?" asked one. Her lip was trembling.

I tried to look stern. "Not this time," I told her. "But — "

"Oh, thank you, thank you, thank you!" she cried.

The girl and her friend hung back. They

watched Addie and me for a moment. Then one of them said shyly, "My name is Shawn Volk. What is yours?"

"Karen Brewer," I told her. "And this is Addie Sidney."

"I'm Becky," said the other girl.

Three other kindergarteners joined Shawn and Becky. Becky whispered to them, "She caught us running, but she did not report us." (Becky was pointing to me.)

"Really?" they said.

Before Addie and I knew what had happened, the little kids had crowded around us.

"Look, I have a loose tooth," said one.

"I got new sneakers," said another.

"My baby brother threw up this morning," said a third.

Addie and I had a great time with the kindergarteners. We talked with them. We acted as grown-up as we could. Finally, the bell rang. I sighed with happiness. This was the job for me, all right.

Great-Grandma's Ring

That afternoon, Addie and I were at our post five minutes before the bell rang. We worked until it was time for our buses to leave. (Mostly we played with Shawn and her friends.)

When my bus stopped at the end of my street, Nancy and Bobby Gianelli and I hopped off.

" 'Bye!" Nancy and I called to Bobby.

"See you!" he called back.

"Karen, can you come over this afternoon?" Nancy wanted to know.

"I think so. I have to check with Mommy."

Mommy said I could. Soon I was in Nancy's room. We sat on her bed. We sat side by side. I saw a pile of magazines at the end of the bed.

"What are those?" I asked.

"Fashion magazines," said Nancy. She handed me one. "See? Big girls look at them and see pictures of clothes they want to wear. And hair styles and stuff. Here is my favorite outfit. If Mommy and Daddy would let me wear it, I would look *so* grown-up." Nancy showed me a picture of a girl wearing a wild black dress with pink cowboy boots.

"And this," Nancy went on, "is my most favorite haircut."

Nancy pointed to a girl with short hair. I decided I did not like the outfit, but I liked the haircut.

"Are you really going to get your hair cut?" I asked.

Nancy shrugged. "If I am allowed." She

jumped off the bed and opened her dresser drawer. She took out a small velvet jewelry box.

"What is that?" I asked her.

"My great-grandma's ring," Nancy replied. "It was her *wedding* ring." Nancy showed me the gold band. "Daddy gave it to me. He said it is mine now. I can wear it on special occasions. It fits my thumb. But you know what?" She sighed. "I asked if I can wear it to school and he said no, I am not old enough. But I know I *am* old enough, Karen. Why won't Mommy and Daddy believe me?"

I shook my head. Who can figure out parents? Then I said, "Want to have a Lovely Ladies tea party?"

"Yeah!" replied Nancy. So we did.

The Accident

On Wednesday, I had a bad day at school. Here is the very first thing that happened after Ms. Colman had taken roll. She said, "Girls and boys, I have an announcement."

Somehow I just knew it was not going to be a wonderful Surprising Announcement. It was not even going to be a good announcement.

"In two weeks," my teacher went on, "you will be taking a test. It is called the two-AT. That means an achievement test for second-graders. All the second-graders here at Stoneybrook Academy will be taking it then."

"How long will it last?" Addie wanted to know.

"Just an hour each morning for three mornings," Ms. Colman replied.

"Do we have to study for it?" Chris asked.

My teacher shook her head. "No. The test is supposed to measure what you know with*out* studying."

"Goody," said Chris.

"So I do not want any of you to worry about the test," Ms. Colman went on. "You cannot fail it. It will just show me what you know."

Do not worry. Do not worry. Guess what. I was already worried. I do not like taking tests. Once, our class had to take some math tests. They were very, very hard for me. So I began copying from Ricky's paper. Then I lied and told Ms. Colman I was *not* copying. I felt horrible. And I got into a lot of trouble. Now I had to take the stupid 2AT. Boo and bullfrogs.

The next bad thing happened after school. It happened while Addie and I were on patrol duty. We were in charge of our hallway intersection as usual. Guess what. I had gotten my wish. Addie and I were the most popular patrols in the Red Brigade. This was because we never reported anybody for doing anything. Sometimes we called out, "Walk, don't run!" or "Take turns at the water fountain!" But that was about it. The kids loved us. Especially the kindergarteners. The big kids kind of liked us, too, since we let them do whatever they wanted.

"Hi, Karen! Hi, Addie!" called a little kid named Fred. He was one of Shawn's friends. "Look. I got a star on my worksheet."

Addie and I peered at Fred's paper. He had gotten a star for matching pictures of things that belong together.

"That is terrific, Fred," said Addie.

"Fantastic," I added.

Three fourth-graders ran by us then.

"No running!" called Addie.

"Okay!" they shouted. They did not slow down.

Addie turned back to Fred. I was waving to Nancy down the hall. And that was when I heard it — little feet running (patter, patter, patter), then a thud, then, "Wah!"

It was Becky. She had run around a corner and smacked into Shawn. She had cut her lip and it was bleeding.

Mrs. Noonan was there in a flash. (Becky has a loud voice.) After she helped Becky to the nurse, she returned to Addie and me. "I understand Becky was running through the hall," she said.

"Well — " I started to answer.

"Girls, you must take your job seriously. You must pay attention at all times. Do you understand?"

"Yes," replied Addie and I.

"And I must tell you something. I am concerned because since you became patrols you have not reported a single student. I do not expect you to be tattletales, but I find it hard to believe that not one student has broken a single rule. So once again, I ask you to take your job seriously. I hope you understand me."

Uh-oh.

Spies

Addie and I talked on the phone that night. We talked for a long time.

"Mrs. Noonan is right, Karen," Addie said. "We are not doing our jobs."

"I know," I replied. I sighed. "But I want the kids to like us."

"Well, we do not have to be mean to them."

"Addie, no matter how nice we are, they will not like us if we report them," I pointed out.

"But if we do not report a few kids, Mrs.

Noonan is going to talk to us again. I do not want that."

So Addie and I agreed on something. And we tried it out the next morning. As soon as Addie and I reached our post, a girl walked by us. She dropped a candy wrapper on the floor.

"No littering!" I called. Then I added, "This is your first warning. If we catch you again, we will report you."

"You will?' said the girl.

"Yes," I replied. And I meant it.

A moment later, Becky ran by us. "Hey, Becky! No running!" said Addie. Then she added, "You really cannot run anymore. That is how you got hurt yesterday. I am not going to report you now. But if you run again, I will."

"Hmphh," said Becky. But she walked slowly into her classroom.

Addie nudged me then. "Karen," she whispered, "see those two girls?" Addie was pointing to some fifth-graders. They were standing by the door to a classroom.

They were not breaking any rules.

"Yeah?" I said.

"Yesterday afternoon I saw them come out of a fourth-grade room. It was while Mrs. Noonan was talking to us. I wonder what they were doing."

"Hmm. You know what? Last week I saw them go into a kindergarten room. I thought they were going to walk one of the kids home, but they came out alone."

"I wonder why," said Addie. "Why are they going into all these classrooms?"

I frowned. Then I grabbed Addie's sleeve. "Hey! You know what? I bet they are the ones who are stealing things from everyone's desks and cubbies. They are the crooks!"

"Oh, Karen. You do not know that," said Addie. "You do not have any proof."

"Then let's get proof. Let's spy on them."

"Well . . . okay," said Addie.

The next morning we kept our eyes open. We were looking for the girls. When we saw them, we watched them enter a classroom. It was their own room. But soon they came out into the hall again. They peered into a third-grade room. They tiptoed inside. They came out a few minutes later. They were whispering and giggling. But we did not know if they had stolen anything. So we watched them that afternoon, and again on Monday.

I guess we kind of forgot about our patrol duties. We were so busy watching the girls that we did not notice who was running or fighting or teasing or littering.

Mrs. Noonan reminded us.

"Karen, Addie," she said. "I have been watching you. You are not paying attention to the hallways at all. I do not know what you are doing, but it certainly is not your jobs. If I have to talk to you one more time about this, then I will also ask you to give up your badges. You will have to leave the Red Brigade."

Yikes. I certainly did not want that. And I did not want to miss that badge ceremony. That would be a disgrace.

Nancy's Haircut

"Karen! Karen!" said Nancy the next morning. She was running across her yard to my house. It was time for us to walk to the bus stop. "Guess what! Mommy and Daddy said I can get my hair cut! I showed them the picture from the magazine. The picture of the haircut I like. And they said okay. I can get my hair cut that way. Mommy even made an appointment for me."

"Not at Gloriana's House of Hair," I said.

Nancy looked horrified. "Of *course* not,"

she replied. "At Hair Fair. I am going this afternoon. And Mommy said you and Hannie can come with me. Won't that be fun?"

"Cool," I said.

The only thing that was not cool was that Hannie could not come after all. She was going shopping with her mother.

"I cannot wait to see you tomorrow," she called to Nancy as we left school. "Good luck."

Mrs. Dawes drove Nancy and Danny and me downtown. Danny is Nancy's baby brother. And I mean he is her *baby* brother. He is only a few months old. I like everything about him except his diapers.

We parked in front of Hair Fair. We walked inside. Nancy was holding the magazine picture. It was kind of smudged and crumpled, but you could still see the haircut.

Nancy marched up to the counter. "Hello. My name is Nancy Dawes," she said importantly. "I have a four-thirty appointment. I want my hair to look just like this." She held out the picture.

"Well, we will see what we can do," said the woman behind the counter. She gave Nancy a blue smock to wear over her clothes. "Your hairdresser will be Emilia, and she will be with you very soon."

Nancy sat down in the special haircutting chair. She swung her feet back and forth. Then I spun her around for awhile.

Finally Emilia stepped over to us. "Hi, there," she said.

"Hi," we replied. And Nancy said, "Can you cut my hair just like this?" She remembered to add, "Please?"

"Certainly," said Emilia. "First, Caitlin will wash your hair."

Nancy left with Caitlin. When she came back, her hair was wet.

Snip, snip, snip. The scissors clipped away. Nancy's hair fell to the floor, bit by bit. At first I closed my eyes. I just could not help thinking about Gloriana's House of Hair. I did not want Nancy to look like a squirrel, too. But when I opened my eyes,

I smiled. Nancy smiled back at me in the mirror.

Her hair looked great so far.

Emilia saw us smiling at each other. "What do you think?" she asked.

"Great," I said.

"Perfect," said Nancy.

Her long hair was getting shorter and shorter. Soon it was shorter than Hannie's. (But not as short as my squirrel haircut.)

Finally Emilia said, "There you go, hon. A good old-fashioned pageboy. Your hair will look even prettier when your bangs grow out a little."

Nancy and I did not know what a pageboy was. But we did not care. Nancy's hair looked fantastic. And she really did look just like the girl in the magazine. Also, she looked older.

"How much older?" Nancy asked me as we were leaving.

"At least nine," I replied.

Nancy grinned. "Excellent!" she exclaimed.

Caught

Addie and I did not want to lose our patrol badges. We did not want to be kicked out of the Red Brigade. But we did want to know what those fifth-grade girls were doing.

"I am sure they are the thieves," said Addie.

"Me too," I replied.

"And I want to catch them."

"Me too. I do not think anyone would mind that we spied — if we caught the thieves," I said.

So Addie and I came up with a plan. We decided we would spy one at a time. While Addie spied, I would stay at our patrol post. And while I spied, Addie would stay at our patrol post.

At first we did not see much. But we learned the girls' names. They were Kathy Crawford and Nicole Seegal. Linny Papadakis knew them. (He sounded as if he did not like them very much.)

Then one afternoon, just as patrol duty was about to end, Addie came flying around a corner in her wheelchair. "Karen! Karen!" she cried. "Kathy and Nicole just snuck into another classroom. Come back there with me now. We can catch them in the act!"

I looked up and down the halls. They were just about empty. Most of the kids had left school already. "Well . . . okay," I said.

"Hurry up!" Addie whipped back around the corner. She can go *fast* in that chair.

I ran after her.

Addie came to a sudden stop outside of a third-grade room. I crashed into the back of her chair.

"Shhh!" hissed Addie.

"Sorry," I said. "But you should warn me when you are going to stop."

Addie waved her hand at me to be quiet. Then she pointed into the room. I peeked inside. I saw Kathy and Nicole. They were pawing through the desks in the classroom.

I glanced at Addie. She glanced at me. Then we looked into the room again. And we both saw Nicole reach into some kid's desk, pull out a quarter, and slip it into her pocket.

I sprang into the room.

"Gotcha!" I cried.

I had caught the thieves.

Kathy and Nicole looked up in surprise. Addie wheeled into the classroom behind me. "We know who you are," she said.

"Oh, yeah? Who are we?" replied Nicole. She narrowed her eyes.

"You are Nicole Seegal and Kathy Crawford. You have been stealing stuff from kids' desks and cubbies. The teachers are going to be really glad we found out who you are. You are the Stoneybrook Academy crooks."

"Want to make something of it?" said Nicole.

"We can beat you up," added Kathy.

"Oh, yeah?" replied Addie. But she looked scared.

"Anyway, you do not have any proof that we took things," said Kathy.

"That's right," said Nicole. "If you told the teachers about us, we would just say we did not take anything. We would say you made a mistake. That someone else is the thief. It would be your word against ours."

"Besides," Kathy went on, "if you *do* say anything, Mrs. Noonan will know you were spying instead of doing your jobs. Won't she? Nicole and I heard all about that. And if she thinks you were spying she will take away your badges."

"So you better keep your mouths shut," said Nicole.

"Okay," said Addie and I in small voices.

The 2AT

When I woke up on Wednesday morning, I rolled over and groaned. I did not want to go to school. This was not because of Nicole and Kathy. It was because of the 2AT. We were going to begin the test that day.

"Mommy? I do not feel very well," I said when I sat down to breakfast.

Mommy was busy fixing coffee. She did not even turn around. "I know about the 2AT, Karen," she replied.

"Oh." I poked at my toast. "So I guess I have to go to school."

"Absolutely."

"Boo and bullfrogs," I replied.

Ms. Colman passed around the test papers as soon as she had taken roll. "The first part of the test is vocabulary," she said. "And reading comprehension. It is not very different from the exercises in your workbooks. So listen closely to my directions, and then you may begin. Remember to keep your eyes on your *own* paper." (Ms. Colman glanced at me then.) "And just raise your hand if you are having trouble. I will come to your desk and answer your question."

A few minutes later, Ms. Colman said, "Three, two, one, go." And the test began. I read each question carefully. I read the fill-in-the-blank sentences carefully. I thought before I wrote down any answers. You know what? The butterflies in my tummy went away. The test was not too bad after all. I did not even *think* about looking at Ricky's paper. I was doing fine by myself. Even Ms. Colman thought so. She smiled at me when she collected our test papers.

My classmates and I were very glad when lunchtime came. We hurried to the cafeteria. We needed a break. We ate our lunches. Then we ran onto the playground. Hannie and Nancy and I played hopscotch. We had a lot of energy to get rid of.

When recess was over, we returned to our classroom. We had been there for about one second when I heard Tammy scream.

"Aughh! My Troll is gone!" she cried. "My brand new Troll." Tammy looked as if she were going to cry.

"Are you sure it is gone?" asked Terri.

Tammy nodded. "It was right here in my desk before lunch."

Ms. Colman shook her head. "Not again," she said.

"You should not leave things in your desk anymore," spoke up Natalie. "It is not safe."

"I guess not," replied Tammy. She sniffled.

I glanced at Ms. Colman. She had turned to the blackboard. Her back was facing us. She had not told us to sit down yet.

"Addie," I whispered. "We have to talk."

Addie and I moved to a corner of the room.

"You know who took Tammy's Troll, don't you?" I said.

"Yup. Nicole and Kathy."

I nodded. "I bet they sneak into empty classrooms any time they feel like it. Not just after school, but when kids are at lunch or recess, too. They probably say they have to go to the girls' room. Then they look for empty classrooms instead."

"They are so sneaky," said Addie.

"I wonder how long they will do this," I went on. "They could do it forever. None of our stuff would be safe. The teachers are not very good at catching them."

"But what can we do?" asked Addie.

"Tell Mrs. Noonan?" I suggested.

"But then we will lose our badges."

I sighed. "Okay. I guess we have to keep quiet."

Watch Out!

The next day was the second day of the 2AT. I felt just a little nervous at first. Then I relaxed. This time, we had to read paragraphs and stories, then answer questions about them. I am pretty good at that. I decided I would not even worry about the last day of the 2AT, even though the last day was going to be math day.

You will never guess what happened when my classmates and I returned to our room after recess that afternoon. Pamela shrieked, "Oh, no! Someone stole my money! I had a whole dollar."

"Pamela, did you leave money in your desk?" asked Ms. Colman.

"We-ell . . ." Pamela sounded as if she felt a little foolish.

"That was not very smart," said Natalie.

"Unfortunately, we all need to be a bit more careful right now," added Ms. Colman.

Pamela stuck her tongue out at Natalie. Then she turned to Leslie and Jannie. "Darn. I was going to buy a comic book."

Once again I grabbed Addie.

"This is *not fair*," I whispered loudly to her. "You know I do not like Pamela very much. But still — we should be able to leave things in our desks. We should not have to worry."

"I know," replied Addie. She looked at me warily. "Karen, what are you going to do?" she asked. "I can tell you are going to do something."

"I am going to talk to Kathy and Nicole, that's what. I will talk to them after school today. I am going to say that I will tell the teachers I know who the crooks are. Enough is enough."

That afternoon while Addie and I were on patrol duty, I watched for Kathy and Nicole. When I saw them, I said to Addie, "Okay, you are in charge. I will be right back."

Kathy and Nicole were leaving their classroom. I marched up to them. "Halt," I said sternly.

"Make us," replied Kathy.

I pointed to my badge. "I am a patrol."

Kathy and Nicole halted. "What do you want?" asked Nicole.

"I want to talk to you. In private."

The girls rolled their eyes. Kathy let out an enormous sigh. "Oh, all right," she said. "Let's go back to our room. No one is in there now." She spun around.

Nicole and I followed her. The three of us stood just inside the doorway. "So talk," said Nicole.

I cleared my throat. "Um, all right. Yes-

terday someone stole a Troll out of Tammy Barkan's desk. And today someone stole a dollar out of Pamela Harding's desk."

"So?" said Kathy.

"So I think you did it."

"Did you see us?" asked Nicole.

"Can you prove it?" asked Kathy.

I squirmed. "No. . . . But I know you did it anyway. I am going to tell the teachers."

"We will say we did not do it," said Kathy.

"And I have a suggestion for you," added Nicole.

"What is it?" I asked.

"How about if you leave us alone?"

"But — " I started to say.

"Or we will beat you up," Nicole went on. "Understand? The two of us. We will *beat you up*. So do not open your mouth."

I looked at the girls. They were bigger than me. They were taller than me. They were tougher than me. "Okay," I replied. I backed out of the classroom.

Nancy's Mistake

Friday.

I was happy when I woke up on Friday morning. I was looking forward to the weekend. Mommy and Seth were going out on Saturday night, and Kristy was going to baby-sit for Andrew and me. On Sunday, Hannie and Nancy and I were planning to roller-skate.

Another good thing about Friday was that it was the last day of the 2AT. I was not even nervous about it anymore.

Nancy was even more excited about Friday than I was. In the morning she ran out of her house with a big smile on her face.

"Notice anything new?" she asked me.

"Not your hair," I said. Nancy's haircut was a week and a half old.

"Oh, no. Much newer than that."

I looked at Nancy from the top of her head all the way down to . . . her feet. "New shoes!" I exclaimed. "You got new shoes!"

"*And* I picked them out my*self*. Mommy did not see them first and say 'How do you like these, Nancy?' *I* saw them and said, 'How do you like these, *Mommy*?' And she said, 'They are fine.' So we bought them."

Nancy's new shoes were very cool and *very* grown-up.

We walked toward the bus stop. Nancy was still smiling.

"Now what?" I asked her.

"Notice anything else?"

Something else? I looked at Nancy again. This time I could not see another new thing. "Well, no," I had to say.

Nancy held out her hand. On her thumb was her great-grandmother's ring. "Awesome! Your parents let you wear it to school?" I exclaimed.

"Yup. They said they trust me. They said I really am growing up."

This was very important news.

And Nancy certainly felt important. She showed her ring and her new shoes to everybody at school that morning.

When lunchtime came, I let out a yelp. The 2AT was over! I had finished it, and it had not scared me, and I had not copied. My classmates and I rushed through lunch so we could play outside. On the playground, Nancy and Hannie and I built a snowman. We invented a game called Slush Race. We were out of breath when we returned to our classroom.

Hannie and Nancy headed for their desks in the back of the room. I sat down at my desk in the front of the room.

"Oh, no!" I heard someone cry.

I turned around. It was Nancy.

"What's wrong?" Hannie was asking her.

"My ring! My ring is gone!"

I ran to my friends. "Your ring? How did you lose it?" I asked.

Nancy shook her head. "I didn't lose it. Exactly. I left it right here in my desk. I took it off before we went to the cafeteria, because I was afraid I would lose it on the playground when we were running around. I was trying to be responsible." Nancy began to cry.

I did not say to Nancy, "But you *know* someone has been stealing stuff out of desks." I could see that Nancy felt bad enough already. Instead, I told Nancy to tell Ms. Colman. Then I found Addie. "We have to talk," I said to her. "We have to do something about Kathy and Nicole. They stole Nancy's ring. We have to find a way to make the teachers believe us."

"Okay," Addie replied. "How about — "

But just then Mrs. Colman stood up from

her desk. She clapped her hands. "Back to your seats, girls and boys," she said.

"Darn it," said Addie.

"I will talk to you when we have our break," I whispered to Addie. Then I scurried to my desk.

The Sneaky Plan

Addie and I had a lot to do on our break. We needed to make an important plan, and we did not have much time. As soon as our break began, I ran to Addie. She scooted into a corner, and we talked there.

"We have to catch them," I said to Addie. "We have to catch Kathy and Nicole. And we have to do it today."

"Why do we have to do it today?" asked Addie.

"Because we cannot let them keep stealing things anymore. Nancy is going to be in big trouble over her ring. And she did not do a thing wrong. Nicole and Kathy are the ones who should be in trouble."

"But if we catch them, Mrs. Noonan will know we were spying. She will know we were not doing our jobs. We will lose our badges."

I sighed. "I know. But . . . but maybe that is not as important as stopping the crooks." I turned toward the back of the classroom. I looked at Nancy. She was sitting at her desk crying.

Addie looked back at her, too. "I guess you are right," she said.

"The hard part," I went on, "is that we have to have *proof* that Kathy and Nicole are stealing. How will we get proof?"

"What if a teacher saw them stealing?" suggested Addie.

"Hey! That is a great idea!" I cried. I thought for a moment. Then I said slowly, "What if Kathy and Nicole thought they would find something great somewhere — like here in our classroom?" I paused. I was thinking of a very good plan. Addie looked at me impatiently. Finally, I said, "Okay, how about this? How about if we let Kathy and Nicole think that Bobby or someone is keeping a Walkman in his desk. We can have a really loud conversation about it so they will be sure to hear us. Then we will say that Ms. Colman will leave school at three-thirty this afternoon. So Kathy and Nicole will be sure to sneak into our room right after Ms. Colman leaves."

"But if Ms. Colman leaves, how will she catch them?"

"Okay. You and I will be waiting for Ms. Colman outside the front door. We will tell her to go back to our room. When she does, she will find Kathy and Nicole looking through our desks."

Addie's eyes lit up. "Oh, cool! I get it!" she said. "That is a super plan, Karen. There is just one problem. If we stay after school until three-thirty, we will miss our buses."

"Hmm. Okay. Let me see. All right, I will ask Nancy to tell my mom I went home with you on your bus. Then Mommy will not worry. At least not too much. And Addie, you tell — "

"Wait," Addie interrupted me. "I cannot say I am going home on your bus. My wheelchair could not go on your bus. That is why I ride the special bus. It is just for kids in wheelchairs."

Now that was a problem. But after a few moments, Addie said, "I know. My mom will not be home this afternoon until my bus drops me off. So while we are on patrol duty, I will call my house. I will leave a message on the answering machine saying we have a special Red Brigade meeting this afternoon, and I have to stay for it. I will ask my mom to pick me up at school at four o'clock. Then she will not worry, either."

"Perfect," I said. "Now we have to make sure we see Kathy and Nicole while we are on duty. And they believe our story."

"Boy, I hope our plan works," said Addie.

"Me too. But what could go wrong?"

"Everything," replied Addie.

Trouble

Right off the bat, things did not go the way we had planned.

I said to Nancy, "Addie and I have thought of a way to catch the crooks. But we will have to stay after school to do it. We will have to miss our buses. I do not want Mommy to worry when I do not get off the bus. So can you please tell her I went home with Addie?"

Nancy looked uncomfortable. "That would be lying," she said.

"But I am trying to catch the crooks."

"But *I* am trying to be more grown-up. I do not think I should lie."

"*Please*, Nancy? Just this once. It is not a huge lie."

"Maybe," said Nancy.

I would have to live with that. I could not worry about what Nancy was going to do. I had too many other things to think about.

As soon as Addie and I left our classroom for patrol duty, Addie wheeled herself to the pay phone in the hallway. She called her house and left the message for her mother. Then she told one of the other kids who rides her bus to tell the driver not to wait for her.

"Great," I said. "That was Part One of our plan. Now for Part Two."

Part Two was to find Nicole and Kathy and let them know that a Walkman was in Bobby Gianelli's desk. (This was not true, but it didn't matter. We just wanted to make sure Kathy and Nicole would have a reason to root through the desks in our classroom.)

Addie kept her eye out for the thieves. She spotted them just as patrol duty was ending. We hurried to the classroom they had snuck into. We stopped just outside the door. Then I said to Addie in a very loud voice, "Can you believe Bobby brought his new *Walkman* to school?"

"No. That was *so silly*," Addie replied, just as loudly. "It will be stolen for sure."

"He left it *right* in his *desk!*" I added. "*Over* the *week*end."

"Well, at least it will be safe until *three-thirty*."

"Yeah. Ms. Colman has to stay until *three-thirty* to grade the 2AT tests. But then she has to *leave*."

"Well, come on," said Addie. "We better go or we will miss our buses."

Addie and I hurried off. We had already missed our buses and we knew it. Now came the boring part of the plan. Waiting for three-thirty. That was almost half an hour away. And we had to wait where no one would see us. This was not easy with Addie's wheelchair. But I found a spot by the front door behind some bushes. The ground was hard because it was so cold. I rolled Addie's chair in there easily. We talked and tried to keep warm.

We were waiting for Ms. Colman to come out.

After awhile I looked at my watch. "Three-thirty," I said to Addie.

"She should be here any minute now," Addie replied.

Soon we heard footsteps in the hallway. *Click, click, click.* And then Ms. Colman walked out the front door.

I stepped in front of her.

"Karen!" exclaimed Ms. Colman. Then she saw Addie in the bushes. "What on earth — " she started to say.

But I had to interrupt her. "Ms. Colman, I will explain everything later," I said in a hurry. "Right now, can you come back to

84

the classroom with Addie and me? It is really important."

"Well . . . sure."

The three of us rushed back inside and down the hallway. We paused in the doorway to our room. There were Nicole and Kathy. They were pawing through our desks. I saw Kathy slip something into her pocket.

More Trouble

"Ahem!" Ms. Colman cleared her throat loudly.

Kathy and Nicole both jumped. Kathy tried to take the something out of her pocket. But Ms. Colman stepped forward. "Please give me that," she said. Kathy handed it over.

"Hey!" exclaimed Addie as she wheeled herself into the room. "That is Hannie's new eraser!"

Ms. Colman looked sternly at Kathy and

Nicole. "You have a lot of explaining to do," she said.

This time Kathy and Nicole could not say anything about "our word against theirs." They could not say they were not the thieves. A grown-up had caught them stealing.

So what did Kathy say then? She said, "Here. Take the stupid old eraser." And she threw it at Addie.

"I do not know how you two knew these girls were in our room," Ms. Colman started to say to Addie and me, "but — "

We were interrupted then. We were interrupted by my mother and Mrs. Sidney. They dashed into the room.

"Karen!" said Mommy.

"Addie!" said Mrs. Sidney.

Then at the same time they said, "Thank goodness you are all right."

"How did you know we were here?" I asked.

"Nancy came to me with a very strange

story after she got off the bus," said Mommy. "Something about your going to Addie's house, but not really. And you were not on the bus. So I called Mrs. Sidney."

"And I had just found your message on the answering machine," Mrs. Sidney said to Addie. "We did not know *what* was going on. We called Mrs. Noonan. We called Mrs. Titus. We — "

At that moment, Mrs. Noonan and Mrs. Titus ran into the room.

"You are in big trouble, Karen," Mommy said to me.

"So are you," Mrs. Sidney said to Addie.

"Now just a minute, please," said Ms. Colman. "I am not sure how they did it, but somehow, Karen and Addie caught the thieves."

"What thieves?" asked Mommy.

Addie and I had a lot of explaining to do ourselves.

Heroes

Nicole and Kathy were in Very Big Huge Trouble. Addie and I were just in big trouble. Our parents were angry. They were happy that we had caught the crooks, but they were not happy about the way we had done it.

"You asked Nancy to lie for you," Mommy said to me.

"You really did lie to me," Mrs. Sidney said to Addie.

"You made us sick with worry," said Mommy.

"We did not know where you were or what you were doing," said Mrs. Sidney. "We did not know if you were safe."

Addie and I were both punished. That night Mommy and Seth said, "No TV for a week." Mr. and Mrs. Sidney said, "You are grounded in your bedroom for the entire weekend."

Boo and bullfrogs.

Still, I knew our parents were proud of what we had done.

Better yet, on Monday the kids at school called us heroes.

"Now we can keep things in our desks again," said Bobby.

"We will not have to worry," said Natalie.

Even better, Nancy was going to get her ring back. A bunch of kids were going to get their things back. Kathy and Nicole had eaten the candy they had taken. And they had spent the money they had taken. But the rest of the things were in their bedrooms.

Best of all, Mrs. Noonan let Addie and me keep our patrol badges. She did not kick us out of the Red Brigade. We went back to our job in the hallway intersection.

Kathy tried to make her kick us out, though. On that Friday when we found Kathy and Nicole in our classroom, Kathy said to Mrs. Noonan, "You ought to fire them as patrols! They were not doing their jobs! You know how they found out about us? They were spying. They were spying when they were supposed to be on patrol duty. You should take away their badges."

But Mrs. Noonan just smiled at Addie and me. "Take away their badges? I do not think so. They may be two of our best patrols ever. I asked them to pay attention to what was going on, and they certainly did."

Addie and I grinned at Kathy and Nicole then. Kathy and Nicole just glared at us. Nicole even stuck out her tongue.

There was one thing I did not understand. "Mommy?" I said later that night. "Why did Nicole and Kathy take all those things? They did not really need them. And they have allowance money to spend. So why were they stealing?"

Mommy and Seth and I were sitting on the couch. Mommy took my hand. "I think they were stealing because they are not very happy," she told me.

I looked up at her. "I don't get it."

"Well," said Mommy, "maybe they are having some trouble in school. Or maybe they are having some trouble at home. They probably wanted someone to notice. They wanted their teachers and parents to give them some help. So they did something to attract everyone's attention."

"Oh," I said. "I see."

"That is not the best way to ask for help," Seth pointed out. "But sometimes people think it is the only way."

"Oh," I said again. I felt sorry for Kathy and Nicole. But I was still glad we had caught them.

The Ceremony

Kathy's and Nicole's parents made them give back all the things they had stolen (except, of course, for the candy they ate and the money they spent). And they made them do it in person.

One morning Kathy and Nicole stepped into my classroom. Each of them was holding something in her hand. Kathy looked around the room. She spotted Tammy. She called her over. Then she opened her hand.

"Here is your Troll," she said. "I am sorry we took it."

Nicole called to Nancy. She held out her hand. "Here is your ring," she said. "I am sorry we took it."

Nancy peered at the ring. "Thanks," she said.

Nicole and Kathy left the room. Nancy ran to Hannie and me. "I am so glad I got it back!" she cried. "I will never wear it to school again. Even though I did not get in trouble when it was stolen."

Nancy's parents had been very nice about the missing ring. After all, they had *said* she could wear it to school. And they agreed that Nancy had been responsible when she left it in her desk instead of wearing it on the playground. But all the Daweses agreed that school was not the best place for a special ring.

Remember the bad day I had? The day when I found out about the 2AT, and then Addie and I got in trouble with Mrs. Noonan? Well, a week after Nicole and Kathy were caught, I had a day that was just the opposite. It was terrific!

It was the day of the badge ceremony.

Late in the morning, Ms. Colman said, "Karen, Addie, Vicky, and Terri, it is time for you to go to the auditorium." (Vicky and Terri were going to be the new patrols from our classroom.)

Addie and I grinned at each other. We were wearing our best clothes — birthday party clothes. And as we were on our way to the auditorium, we put on our patrol badges one last time.

"How do I look?" Addie asked me.

"Very official," I replied. "How do I look?"

"Also very official."

In the auditorium were Mrs. Noonan, Mrs. Titus, the new and old patrols, and a lot of mothers and fathers and grandparents. The mothers and fathers and grandparents were sitting in the audience. The patrols were gathering on the stage. Mr. and Mrs. Sidney lifted Addie and her wheelchair on the stage, too. I stood beside

Addie. Then Mrs. Titus stepped up to a microphone.

"Welcome," she said. "Today's program is to honor . . ."

While Mrs. Titus spoke, I looked into the audience. In the second row I saw Mommy and Seth. In the fourth row I saw Daddy and Elizabeth and Nannie and Emily. I smiled at them.

Mrs. Titus finished speaking. Before I knew it, I was walking across the stage and putting my belt and badge on Vicky Anders. Then Addie put her belt and badge on Liddie Yuan from Mr. Berger's class.

When all the badges had been handed over, the audience began to clap. I looked at my parents and Nannie. They were smiling so widely I thought their cheeks would break. And Mommy cried a little.

Later, when the badge ceremony was over, I walked through the hall with Mommy and Seth. It was lunchtime. We ran into Ms. Colman. "Hello!" she greeted them. "I am glad I saw you. I was going to call you this afternoon to tell you how well Karen did on the 2AT. One of the highest scores in the class."

Mommy and Seth hugged me then. "Honey, we are *so* proud of you," said Mommy.

You know what? I was proud of myself, too.

About the Author

ANN M. MARTIN lives in New York City and loves animals, especially cats. She has two cats of her own, Mouse and Rosie.

Other books by Ann M. Martin that you might enjoy are *Stage Fright*; *Me and Katie (the Pest)*; and the books in *The Baby-sitters Club* series.

Ann likes ice cream and *I Love Lucy*. And she has her own little sister, whose name is Jane.

Little Sister

Don't miss #58

KAREN'S SKI TRIP

"Sweaters. I will need lots of sweaters," I said. I found four big ones. As soon as they were in my suitcase, there was not much room for anything else.

"You are not going to go skiing, are you?" said Hannie. "I hear it can be pretty dangerous."

"That is true," said Nancy. "A man at my father's office broke his leg. And he was a really good skier."

"He must *not* have been such a good skier. If he was he would not have broken his leg," I replied.

"I do not know about that," said Hannie. "I hear about a lot of accidents when people go skiing."

"I am not going to have any accidents," I said. "I am very good at ice skating. I am very good at gymnastics. I am sure I will be very good at skiing too."

Little Sister

by Ann M. Martin

author of The Baby-sitters Club®

More Titles... ➡

❑	MQ48231-9	#59	Karen's Leprechaun	$2.95
❑	MQ48305-6	#60	Karen's Pony	$2.95
❑	MQ48306-4	#61	Karen's Tattletale	$2.95
❑	MQ48307-2	#62	Karen's New Bike	$2.95
❑	MQ25996-2	#63	Karen's Movie	$2.95
❑	MQ25997-0	#64	Karen's Lemonade Stand	$2.95
❑	MQ25998-9	#65	Karen's Toys	$2.95
❑	MQ26279-3	#66	Karen's Monsters	$2.95
❑	MQ26024-3	#67	Karen's Turkey Day	$2.95
❑	MQ26025-1	#68	Karen's Angel	$2.95
❑	MQ26193-2	#69	Karen's Big Sister	$2.95
❑	MQ26280-7	#70	Karen's Grandad	$2.95
❑	MQ26194-0	#71	Karen's Island Adventure	$2.95
❑	MQ26195-9	#72	Karen's New Puppy	$2.95
❑	MQ26301-3	#73	Karen's Dinosaur	$2.95
❑	MQ26214-9	#74	Karen's Softball Mystery	$2.95
❑	MQ69183-X	#75	Karen's County Fair	$2.95
❑	MQ69184-8	#76	Karen's Magic Garden	$2.95
❑	MQ69185-6	#77	Karen's School Surprise	$2.99
❑	MQ69186-4	#78	Karen's Half Birthday	$2.99
❑	MQ69187-2	#79	Karen's Big Fight	$2.99
❑	MQ69188-0	#80	Karen's Christmas Tree	$2.99
❑	MQ69189-9	#81	Karen's Accident	$2.99
❑	MQ69190-2	#82	Karen's Secret Valentine	$3.50
❑	MQ69191-0	#83	Karen's Bunny	$3.50
❑	MQ69192-9	#84	Karen's Big Job	$3.50
❑	MQ69193-7	#85	Karen's Treasure	$3.50
❑	MQ69194-5	#86	Karen's Telephone Trouble	$3.50
❑	MQ06585-8	#87	Karen's Pony Camp	$3.50
❑	MQ06586-6	#88	Karen's Puppet Show	$3.50
❑	MQ06587-4	#89	Karen's Unicorn	$3.50
❑	MQ06588-2	#90	Karen's Haunted House	$3.50
❑	MQ55407-7		BSLS Jump Rope Pack	$5.99
❑	MQ73914-X		BSLS Playground Games Pack	$5.99
❑	MQ89735-7		BSLS Photo Scrapbook Book and Camera Pack	$9.99
❑	MQ47677-7		BSLS School Scrapbook	$2.95
❑	MQ43647-3		Karen's Wish Super Special #1	$3.25
❑	MQ44834-X		Karen's Plane Trip Super Special #2	$3.25
❑	MQ44827-7		Karen's Mystery Super Special #3	$3.25
❑	MQ45644-X		Karen, Hannie, and Nancy The Three Musketeers Super Special #4	$2.95
❑	MQ45649-0		Karen's Baby Super Special #5	$3.50
❑	MQ46911-8		Karen's Campout Super Special #6	$3.25

Available wherever you buy books, or use this order form.

Scholastic Inc., P.O. Box 7502, Jefferson City, MO 65102

Please send me the books I have checked above. I am enclosing $_____
(please add $2.00 to cover shipping and handling). Send check or money order – no cash or C.O.Ds please.

Name_____Birthdate_____

Address_____

City_____State/Zip_____

Please allow four to six weeks for delivery. Offer good in U.S.A. only. Sorry, mail orders are not available to residents to Canada. Prices subject to change.   BSLS497